Diamond

Díamond

By Suzanne Weyn

Illustrated by Elisabeth Alba

SCHOLASTIC INC.

New York   Toronto   London   Auckland   Sydney
Mexico City   New Delhi   Hong Kong   Buenos Aires

Thanks to Diana Gonzalez
for help in writing this story.
−S. W.

Dedicated to my parents and all the
wonderful professors who helped lead me here.
−E. A.

Library of Congress Cataloging-in-Publication Data is available.

ISBN-13: 978-0-545-12096-8
ISBN-10: 0-545-12096-9

10 9 8 7 6 5 4 3 2 1   09 10 11 12 13/0

Printed in Singapore
First printing, September 2009

Table of Contents

At River Run Ranch

Ava lived next to River Run Ranch. She could see the horses from her front porch. But she was not on her porch much. After school, she was always at the stable.

Ava mucked stalls and pitched in new hay. She gave the horses oats and fresh water. She brushed the horses and walked them after rides or lessons.

"You are my best worker," Ann, the owner, always told Ava with a smile.

"It's fun!" Ava would reply. "I love being with the horses. I'm a barn brat."

"You're not a *brat*," said Ann. "But I am glad you're at my barn."

To thank Ava for her help at the stable, Ann gave Ava lessons. She also let Ava ride the horses. Ava had been riding for four years. She was a good rider.

One day there was a new horse at the stable. "Her name is Diamond," Ann said.

Ava looked at the small chestnut mare with a white diamond-shaped marking on her forehead. Diamond gazed back at Ava. Her neat, small ears turned toward Ava. "I've never seen a horse like her," Ava said. "Is she a special breed?"

"Diamond is an Arabian horse," Ann told her. "Her owner got too old to ride so she gave Diamond to me. Diamond is what we call aged. That means she is an older horse. Looking at her teeth, I would say Diamond is at least sixteen years old."

"Is she too old to ride?" Ava asked.

"Not at all," Ann said. "Arabians are a very smart and loyal breed of horses. In fact, Arabians are one of the most intelligent and sensitive horses there are. Arabians also keep their high energy into their late teens and twenties."

Ava stroked Diamond's neck. Diamond nickered softly.

"Diamond is really sweet and should be a good horse for lessons," Ann said.

"Everyone will love her," Ava agreed.

Taking Care of Diamond

"**H**ave you tried out Diamond for lessons yet?" Ava asked Ann the next day.

"Not yet. I would like you to try her first," Ann replied. "Can you help me?"

"Sure," Ava agreed.

Ann and Ava went to the tack room. "We'll put a foam pad under her saddle," Ann said. "An older horse will enjoy the extra cushioning. And we'll use a nice, soft egg butt snaffle that will be easy on her mouth."

When Diamond was saddled, Ava led her out to the corral. Once she was in the saddle, Ava pressed Diamond's sides with her legs. She clucked gently and Diamond began to walk. A gentle pull on the reins was all it took to turn her.

At Ava's signal, Diamond trotted, and then cantered.

"You ride her well," said Ann, who had been watching on the fence.

"She's been well trained," Ava said.

Later, when Ava picked Diamond's hoof clean, she saw that Diamond didn't lift her hoof as high as the other horses.

"She's a little stiff because of her age," Ann said. "You'll have to bend and help her a bit more than usual."

The next day, Ava helped with lessons. Ann asked Ava to help a girl named Megan saddle up Diamond. "You'll like Diamond," Ava said as they entered the stable.

Megan made a face when she saw Diamond. "She looks sort of . . . old," she said. For the first time, Ava saw that Diamond's back sagged a tiny bit. She was a little gray around her muzzle and eyes.

"Can I ride Zack instead?" Megan asked, pointing to a gray gelding.

The next person to come for the lesson was a girl named Kit. "Try our new horse, Diamond," Ann said to her.

"You don't want to ride Diamond," Megan told Kit. "She's really old."

"Ann, can I ride a different horse?" Kit asked. "I don't want to ride an old horse. I don't think anyone will."

Old Diamond

By the next lesson, the students had given Diamond a new name. They called her *Old* Diamond. Ava didn't like this new name. "Diamond is young inside," she said to them.

"Then *you* ride her," Megan said. "We want young horses with spirit."

Ava went into the stable to see
Diamond. She stroked Diamond's soft
muzzle. Diamond nickered gently. She
tipped her head down closer to Ava.

Ann came in. "I see the girls don't want
to ride Diamond," she said. "I don't know if I
can keep her if I can't use her for lessons. I
need a lesson horse."

"Then I will ride her!" Ava cried.

The next day, Ava asked Ann if they could take Diamond out on the trail behind the corral. "All right," Ann agreed.

The trail ran along the side of a fast-moving stream. They had to cross a small bridge to the other side. "Rushing water scares some horses," Ann remarked.

"Diamond seems happy to me," Ava said.

"Perhaps she was around water in the past," said Ann. "She has learned that it won't hurt her."

"I bet she knows lots of things that younger horses don't know," Ava said.

Ava rode Diamond a lot in the next two weeks. They got to be the best of friends. Ann went with them on the trail whenever she could. Soon she felt it was safe for Ava and Diamond to take the trail alone.

The Horse Show

One Saturday morning, after lessons, Ann had big news. She gathered all the riders together. "In two weeks, the stable will hold a schooling show."

The riders buzzed with excitement. "What classes will we ride in?" Kit asked.

"I've entered you all in the trail class for starters," Ann replied. "There will be a number of obstacles for you and your horse to pass and challenges to accomplish. I'll post the course on the stable door so you can practice.

"I will put the horses' names in my helmet and you will pick a horse to ride," said Ann.

"Don't put Old Diamond's name in there," Kit said. "No one will want to ride her."

"*I* want her," Ava spoke up.

Ava went inside and saddled Diamond. "Don't you worry," she said to Diamond. "We're going to win the trail class." But deep down, Ava was worried. What if Diamond really was too old to win?

Ava patted Diamond. "Let's start practicing, girl."

The Big Day

The day of the show was windy and cool. Lots of horse trailers pulled into River Run Ranch. Soon there were horses and riders everywhere.

Ava sat back in her saddle. She looked over the course. "Come on, Diamond! You can do it, girl!"

A trail had been set up inside the ring.
A small bridge had been built between posts.
There was a gate with a latch and a mailbox.
There were also two barrels.

Ann reviewed what each rider and horse
would have to do. "You will be judged on how
well your horse behaves, as well as on your
time and your skill," Ann said.

Kit was on a bay gelding named Leo.
She went first. Leo walked to the bridge and
stopped. He seemed afraid to step on it. Kit
urged him on but he wouldn't move.

Next was Megan on Zack. At the gate, Megan asked Zack to halt. He stopped, but as Megan leaned out to try to unlatch the gate, Zack wandered away. Megan almost slid from her saddle.

The third rider's horse knocked over the mailbox. The fourth rider did everything well until she got to the barrels. Her horse refused to back up between them.

Ava and Diamond were the last ones up. Diamond walked across the bridge, moved right to the gate, and waited while Ava unlatched it. Once they were through, she turned and lowered her neck to allow Ava to latch it again. She trotted to the mailbox and waited while Ava put in the letter. Then she backed smoothly between the barrels. Ava knew they had won!

"Diamond, you may be an old horse," she said as the crowd clapped, "but you know what you're doing!"

About the Horse

Facts about Arabians:

1. Arabians are the oldest pure breed. They were known to exist as far back as 2500 B.C.

2. The Arabian excels in long-distance and endurance races.

3. The Arabian breed is known to be very intelligent.

4. Arabian horses love to be with people more than almost any other breed.

5. The average Arabian horse is 14.3 hands, which means it is only four feet, eleven inches high at the shoulders.

When Horses Are All You Dream About...

Visit
www.breyerhorses.com
to get a **FREE**
catalog!

It has to be Breyer® model horses!

Breyer® model horses are fun to play with and collect!
Meet horse heroes that you know and love. Learn about horses
from foreign lands. Enjoy crafts and games.
Visit us at **www.breyerhorses.com**
for horse fun that never ends!